About the Book

Robby Morrison was a nice boy. He always said please and thank you and never interrupted and kept his elbows off the table and put the cap back on the toothpaste and got A in Deportment on his report card and never told a lie—until his ninth birthday. That's when the trouble started.

First of all, his parents gave him a parrot—a parrot that insisted on being called Ivan. Then a girl with purple lipstick made Robby give her his lunch *and* his lunch box. And when Robby came home one day, soaking wet, and explained that a group of boys had pushed him into a puddle...well, his mother and father just didn't believe him anymore!

After a while, even Robby wasn't sure of what's the truth and what's a lie. But with Ivan to help, he found a way to tell the difference, in this humorous, easy-reading story on a subject every child knows.

Ivan the Great

Weekly Reader Books presents

IVAN
THE GREAT

Isabel Langis Cusack

Pictures by Carol Nicklaus

THOMAS Y. CROWELL · NEW YORK

Library of Congress Cataloging in Publication Data

Cusack, Isabel Langis. Ivan the great.
SUMMARY: A parrot named Ivan teaches a nine-year-old
the difference between truth and a lie.
[1. Honesty—Fiction]   I. Nicklaus, Carol.
II. Title.   PZ7.C956Iv   [Fic]   77-26593
ISBN 0-690-03860-7 ISBN 0-690-03861-5 lib. bdg.

To John
&
Perdita Schaffner

CONTENTS

Ivan the Great

OKAY IVAN

Robby Morrison lived at 7 Elm Street with his mother, his father, and his awful older sister, Susan Jane. Robby was a nice boy. He always said please and thank you and never interrupted and kept his elbows off the dinner table and put the cap back on the toothpaste and got A in Deportment on his report card and never told a lie. Except for that time when he was three and bit the mailman on the leg, Robby was just about perfect.

1

2 Okay Ivan

Until his ninth birthday. That was when the trouble started.

It all began as a mistake. On his birthday, his mom and dad gave him a parrot. (He had been going around for weeks saying, "Gee, I wish I had a parrot," and they had gotten the hint. His friend Mickey James had a parrot.) It was Robby's new parrot that started the mix-up.

"What would you like to name him?" Robby's mother asked.

Robby was about to say Polly, not knowing any other names for parrots, but the bird interrupted.

"Ivan," he said.

"Okay," Robby said. "Ivan."

"Okay Ivan?" his father laughed. "That's a strange name for a parrot. Why do you want to name him Okay Ivan?"

"Not Okay Ivan," Robby said. "Just Ivan. He's the one that said it, not me. Didn't you hear him?"

"He did not," Susan Jane said. "He just cleared his throat. He never said a single word."

"He did, too," Robby said, puzzled. "He said, 'Ivan.'"

"Darling, you can name him anything you want

to," his mother said, "but let's not pretend he said something he didn't."

"But I'm not pretending."

"Maybe Robby's joking," his dad said. "Are you joking, son?"

"He said, 'Ivan,' " Robby said, his voice rising.

"He did not," Susan Jane said. "Mom, you ought to wash that child's mouth out with green soap."

"And you ought to shut up," Robby muttered.

"Children!" their mother said. "We are not going to spoil Robby's birthday with a quarrel. We'll call the parrot Ivan. After all, it's Robby's parrot."

"I wasn't pretending," Robby said again.

"Liar!" Susan Jane hissed. Luckily for her, Robby didn't hit girls, or she would have had a black-and-blue life.

When they were alone, Robby asked the parrot if he had said his name was Ivan, but the bird just cocked his head to one side, stared at Robby, and went cluck-cluck. After Robby got into bed that night, he began to wonder if he had made the whole thing up. But he was pretty sure he hadn't.

In the days that followed, Robby spent a lot of time trying to teach Ivan to say, "Polly wants a cracker," but Ivan's only small talk consisted of clucks. The rest of the family gave up trying to educate the bird, but Robby kept on.

"At least Mickey's parrot says one thing," he told Ivan in a moment of discouragement, "even if it's only, 'Boy, have I got a hangover.'"

ROBBY
LOSES HIS
LUNCH
BOX

One day at lunch, Robby was sitting in a swing, un-wrapping his peanut-butter sandwich, when a little girl came up and sat in the next swing. She was wearing purple lipstick and tiny pearl earrings. She drew a grubby-looking jelly doughnut out of a huge paper bag and took a bite.

"Is that all you're going to eat?" Robby asked.

"It's all I got," the little girl said.

"Do you want half my sandwich?"

5

"What kind is it?"

Robby told her, and she took it. Then she looked in his lunch box.

"Can I have the brownie?"

"I guess so," Robby said, and gave it to her.

""That's a nice lunch box," she said, when she had eaten both halves of his sandwich and his brownie and drunk his milk. "Can I have it?"

"No," Robby said. "It's new. I just got it. I lost my old one."

The little girl began to cry in loud wails, and everybody turned and looked. Robby quickly handed her the lunch box. She stopped crying at once and skipped across the playground waving the lunch box in the air. She hadn't even offered him a bite of her jelly doughnut.

"Where's your lunch box?" his mother asked him when he got home from school. "Don't tell me you've lost another one."

"I didn't lose it," Robby said and told his mother about the little girl.

"Who was she?" his mother asked.

"I don't know. I never saw her before."

"What did she look like?"

Robby shrugged. Then he remembered the purple lipstick and the pearl earrings. "She had on lipstick and pearl earrings."

His mother looked at him. "*Lip*stick? And pearl *ear*rings?"

Robby nodded.

"Robby, why don't you come out and say you lost your lunch box again? I won't punish you. Just tell me the truth."

"I *am*!"

"Now I want you to listen to me," his mother said, taking his hand in both of hers. "I don't want you ever, ever, to be afraid to tell me or your dad the truth. If you lose your lunch box, come to us and say, 'I lost my lunch box.' We didn't punish you when you lost your old one, did we? Lying is much worse than losing something. Do you understand?"

"But this time I didn't lose it," Robby said patiently. "I gave it to the little girl."

Suddenly Ivan spoke up. "I believe you."

Robby turned to Ivan in amazement. "So you *can* talk. He can talk, Mom. Did you hear that? He said, 'I believe you.' "

His mother gave him another long look. "Ivan has never said one word since we've had him. He clucked."

"Mom, he didn't cluck. He said, 'I believe you,' plain as day," Robby said.

"I will not have any more of this!" his mother said. "Another word out of you, and I'll have to speak to your father. Lipstick and pearl earrings, and now you tell me Ivan is talking."

"But—"

"That is *enough*, Robert," she said. She only called him Robert when she was pretty mad.

After she had gone upstairs, Robby said to Ivan, "Ivan, did you really believe me?"

Ivan gazed at him but said nothing.

"Polly wants a cracker," Robby said. "If you can say 'I believe you,' you can say 'Polly wants a cracker.'"

"Sure, I can," Ivan said. "But why should I? My name's not Polly, and I hate crackers. Have you got any pizza?"

"I don't think so," Robby said. "Did you really believe me about the little girl?"

"Yes," Ivan said.

"Why?" Robby asked.

"Why not?"

"Thank you, Ivan," Robby said gratefully.

BIG BOYS

A few afternoons later, Robby was walking home from school when a group of big boys came running past him. One of them reached out and pushed him into a puddle. It had rained all day, and the puddle was a big one. The boys all hugged each other and shrieked with laughter as Robby got to his feet, his face red and his pants covered with mud. He said nothing—what was the use?—just slogged on home.

When he told his mother what had happened, she said, "Who were these boys?"

"I don't know," Robby said.

"How many were there?"

"Four. Maybe five. I didn't see."

"In a school the size of Parkhurst Elementary, I should think you'd know everyone. Robby, this isn't like the girl with the pearl earrings, is it? You're not making it up?"

"I told you, some big boys pushed me."

"You didn't trip and fall down?"

"I told you—"

"Remember what I said about lying? Dirty clothes aren't important, Robby, but telling Mother the truth is."

"I believe you," Ivan said, but this time Robby wisely refrained from quoting the parrot.

"Ivan," Robby said later to the bird, "how come nobody believes me any more? They used to."

"*I* believe you," Ivan said. "If you ask me, grown-ups don't trust kids enough. Even a kid has a constitutional right to be presumed innocent until proven guilty. Does that make sense?"

"I don't know, but it sounded good. Maybe if I

could find that little girl or those boys, and bring them home with me, then she'd believe me."

"Fat chance," Ivan said. "You think those kids are coming home with you and admit to being a bunch of stinkers? Forget it. Say, do you want to hear me recite? I can recite 'The Raven' by Edgar Allan Poe. 'Once upon a midnight dreary, while I pondered, weak and weary.' How's that?"

"Is that all of it?"

"Isn't that enough?"

"Where'd you get a name like Ivan?" Robby asked.

"I'm Russian. My whole name is Ivan the Great, but you can call me Ivan."

"Are you lying?" Robby asked.

"That's a white lie," Ivan said, "because I'm a White Russian." He laughed so hard he nearly fell off his perch. When he stopped laughing, he said, "That was a joke."

"What's funny about being Russian?"

Ivan cocked his head to one side and considered. "You know, that's a good question. You've got a mind like a steel trap. Your I.Q. might be higher than mine, but I doubt it. So it wasn't funny. You could have laughed—just common decency."

"Let's get back to lying," Robby said. "I haven't told one single lie—not even a fib—but every time I open my mouth, they think I'm lying."

"It's really my fault," Ivan admitted. "I started it. They thought you made it up when you said I wanted to be called Ivan. And once they think they've caught you in a biggie, it's downhill all the way, brother."

"Maybe I'd be smarter to lie," Robby said. "Then they might believe me."

"I don't recommend it," the parrot said. "Honesty is the best policy. Washington said that in the Gettysburg Address."

"Why is it?" Robby asked.

Ivan looked at him. "I'm not going to tell you. Not that I don't know. Use your head. I got another quote. 'To thine own self be true, and then thou canst not lie to anybody else.' Or words to that effect. You get the drift."

"I like that," Robby said. "Who said it?"

"Edgar Allan Poe. I think. Do you know what it means?"

"No."

"Don't lie to yourself," Ivan said. "*They* think you lied, but *you* know you didn't. That's the important thing. Maybe it was Walter Cronkite. I would have made a great newscaster. I have a beautiful voice."

"When Mom calls me Robert, next comes the spanking," Robby said.

"Dan'l Boone? Moby Dick? Ah well, it'll come to me. 'To thine own self be true.' Spanking or no spanking."

"That's easy for you to say," Robby pointed out. "You're not the one that gets spanked."

Ivan cocked his head. "That kind of logic is hard to fight," he admitted.

FATSO'S BIRTHDAY PARTY

Robby's friend Fatso Cotter was having a birthday. Robby spent what was left of his own birthday money plus his whole allowance on a light for Fatso's bike. He even bought tissue paper and ribbon to wrap it up, and a big, funny card. He knew Fatso was going to have a party because he had already invited Mickey James and two other boys. He wrapped the light and put it in his closet and waited for Fatso to invite him. The morning of

Fatso's birthday Robby took the present to school with him because he was still sure Fatso was going to invite him. He even told his mother he wouldn't be home till dinnertime because he was going to Fatso's party, and she made him wear his good pants.

He saw Fatso three times that day, and Fatso said nothing about the party.

After school Robby walked home very slowly, carrying the present hidden in his new lunch box in case somebody saw it and asked him who it was for. He considered walking by Fatso's house, so Fatso could look out and see him and remember that he'd forgotten to invite him to the party. But his feet didn't turn left on Crescent Circle. They kept going to Elm Street. Robby thought if he walked slowly enough he might not get home till dinnertime, and then he wouldn't have to say he hadn't been invited to the party. But as he opened the door, the clock was striking four.

"Hi," his mother said, looking surprised. Even Ivan looked surprised. "Forget something?"

"No," Robby said.

"Then why aren't you at the party?"

"I—I didn't feel like it."

"Didn't feel like going to a party? My goodness! Come here and let me see if you have a temperature."

"I'm all right," Robby said.

"Why didn't you go?"

Robby started to say, "He didn't ask me," but the words stuck in his throat. As if she had read his mind, his mother said gently, "Were you invited, son?"

"Sure I was invited," Robby heard himself say rather loudly. "He invited me. He invited me *twice*. But I didn't feel like it. I've got this stomach-ache."

"Wow!" Ivan said.

There, Robby thought, now I've done it! He had finally told a real lie. He felt as if his mother had caught him running up and down the street without his clothes on, like that time Susan Jane went out in nothing but her overshoes and her Easter hat.

But his mother didn't even seem mad. She just nodded and said briskly, "Well, I think you'll feel better when you see what we're having for dinner. I'm going right out to the kitchen and make your very favorite apple pie, and I'm going to call Dad and have him bring home some ice cream. Maple walnut. Think you'll feel well enough for apple pie and ice cream?"

Robby managed a dazed nod.

"That wasn't really a lie," he explained to Ivan when his mom was telephoning his father. "It was a—a fib, like."

"Doesn't add up, does it?" Ivan asked. "You tell three whoppers—not one, but *three*—and you get apple pie and ice cream. Not that I'm so crazy about ice cream. I'd prefer cornbread. That's because I used to be a southern Russian."

"*Three* whoppers?" Robby asked, aghast. "I only counted one."

"Three. You said Fatso invited you, which he didn't; and then that he invited you twice, which of course he didn't since he didn't even invite you once. Then you made up the stomach-ache. You don't do things by halves, buddy boy."

"You're right. It was three. And I didn't get caught. I must be a pretty good liar."

"Hold it!" Ivan said. "Don't get a swelled head just yet. Your mom saw through the whole bit, but she didn't want to hurt your pride. When you tell a

lie to save face, as we Japanese say, that's not such a terrible lie."

"I thought you were Russian."

"That was last week."

"I never knew there were different kinds of lies," Robby said.

"Millions," Ivan said. "Even thousands. I forget which is more."

"Millions," Robby said.

"I got it! Shakespeare. He's the one that said, 'To thine own self be true.' Good advice. You want to hear me sing? I learned some swell songs in a saloon in Shanghai. Yes, siree, honesty is the best policy."

"I'm not so sure," Robby said. "All it gets me is in trouble."

THE
RETURN OF
AUSTRALIA

The next day as Robby was starting to eat his lunch with Mickey and some other boys, the little girl with the pearl earrings and lipstick went skipping by, still swinging his lunch box. Robby hastily hid his sandwich and ran after her.

"Hey!" he called. "Little girl! What's your name?"

She turned and looked at him.

"Australia," she said. "What's yours?"

"Robert Edward Morrison. What kind of a name is Australia? What's your last name?"

"That's all. Just Australia. You got any more brownies? Where do you live? What do you have for lunch?"

"No," Robby said. "Seven Elm Street. I ate it already."

She made a hideous face at him and skipped off.

When he got home, he told his mother about seeing the little girl again and that her name was Australia. He was so pleased about having found out her name that it never occurred to him that his mother wouldn't believe him this time.

"*Australia*? Australia what?"

"That's all," Robby said. "Just Australia."

"Did anybody else see her?"

"Well, sure, they must've. She was there."

"Robby," his mother said, "are you making this up?"

"No!"

"Very well. I'm going to call the principal and see if there is any child named Australia at Parkhurst. You can't have any objections if you're telling the truth. Right?"

"I guess so," Robby sighed.

There was no one at Parkhurst Elementary named Australia—the principal laughed when he said it—and that night Robby got a spanking.

"I don't want to do this," his father said, "but you're too old now for fantasizing. Do you know what that means?"

"Lying," Robby said wearily, because he was getting awfully tired of that word.

After the spanking, Robby said to Ivan, "You know I was telling the truth. And where did it get me?"

"You're getting blamed for another person's lie," Ivan said. "It's tough, but that's the way the cookie crumbles, as we French say. I'm thinking of changing my name to Pierre. It suits my personality better."

"You mean that the little girl lied?" Robby asked.

"Of course. No one in their right mind would name a helpless baby Australia."

"She's no helpless baby!"

"Well, she must have been once. She wasn't born with lipstick and earrings."

"Listen," Robby said. "Couldn't *you* tell them I'm not a liar?"

"If it comes to that, I will," Ivan promised.

"If it comes to *what*?"

"Let's see what develops," Ivan said vaguely. "For the moment, just think of me as your ace in the hole. I'd like a good game of seven-card stud. Do you play poker?"

"No. But I can beat Susan Jane at bridge."

"Bridge is a thinking man's game," the parrot said. "I'm a gambling man."

THE
FIGHT

One day a girl in Robby's class brought her pet squirrel to school, and someone let him out of his cage. When the teacher asked who did it, a boy named Foster Kane called, "Robby Morrison." Robby hadn't done it, and when school let out, he chased Foster across the playground, caught him, and punched him in the mouth. It turned into a scuffle, and when Mr. Hotchkiss, the English teacher, separated them, Robby had a torn sweater

and a collection of cuts, scrapes, and bruises.

"Don't you ever speak to me again," Foster shouted.

"I wouldn't speak to you if you was the last person on earth," Robby shouted back.

"*Were* the last person on earth," Mr. Hotchkiss said. "Now you boys—"

"If I was the last person on earth, you wouldn't *be* on earth, so you couldn't speak to me anyways, smarty," Foster shouted even louder.

"Now, now, that's enough," Mr. Hotchkiss said. "You both go straight home, and I'll talk to you in the morning."

When Robby got home, he was doing his best not to cry because his skinned knee was hurting and his elbow felt as if it might be broken.

When his mother saw him, she cried, "What happened to you?"

Robby hesitated. He'd been told often enough how his parents felt about fighting. It was even worse than lying, and he'd had enough punishment for one day.

"I fell down," he said.

There was a single cluck from Ivan.

"Oh, your poor knee," his mother said. "Come, I'll put something on it."

As she was swabbing his knee and he was trying not to wince, she said, "Robby, you weren't *fighting*, were you?"

"Ouch!" Robby said. "No, ma'am."

"I'm thankful for that," his mom said. "Is that better? I'll bet you could use a cup of hot chocolate. That must have been some fall."

"Oh, it wasn't so bad," Robby said bravely.

But Susan Jane came home with a different story. It hadn't crossed Robby's mind that bad news travels fast, even as far as the sixth grade.

"Did he tell you what he did, Mom?" she asked before she was halfway in the door. "He got into a fight with Candy Kane's kid brother. Robby hit him first. All kinds of kids saw it."

"Her I could live without," Ivan muttered. As usual, no one but Robby heard him.

That night after a long heart-to-heart, man-to-man talk with his father, Robby asked the parrot,

"Ivan, what's a compulsative liar?"

"Compulsive," Ivan corrected. "*K-u-m*—ah well, spelling's not my bag. Is that what he called you?"

Robby nodded.

"If you're a compulsive liar, I'm Snow White and the Seven Dwarfs," Ivan said. "A compulsive liar is someone who lies just for the sake of lying. You don't do that. Listen, I'm not knocking your folks, but they're only human. They make mistakes, and your father's made a beaut. Let's analyze this step by step. You lied about the fight. Why?"

"I don't know."

"*Never* hand me any I don't knows," Ivan ordered. "That's the lazy man's answer, and you're a thinking man. Why did you lie about the fight?"

"I knew I'd get a spanking if I told the truth."

"But you didn't get a spanking."

"I got a talking-to," Robby said. "That's practically as bad."

"Okay. You lied because you didn't want a spanking. Not a good reason, but it's better than none. What else?"

"Three lies about Fatso's birthday party."

"They were to save your pride," Ivan said. "There again, not the best of reasons. But compulsive? No way. Did I tell you I had a degree in psychology? Forget that. It's a you-know-what. Any more lies?"

"Well, I did tell Australia I'd eaten my lunch, and I'd only taken one bite. But I had to lie, or she'd have started bawling again."

Ivan waited.

Finally Robby said, "All right, I guess I could have told her the truth and then run away."

"Mind like a steel trap," Ivan said. "Now you've got your head on straight."

"Ivan," Robby said, "how come you believe me even when you know I'm lying?"

"Because I know you're only lying on the *outside*," Ivan said. "Inside, you're as truthful as I am, and that's a lot of truthful, you'd better believe. Does that make sense?"

"No," Robby said.

"Ah well, so what? Why does everything have to make sense? It was a beautiful thought. I may put it on my Christmas cards."

"Dad said I'm not to be trusted," Robby said gloomily.

"*I* trust you," the parrot said. "With my life. Or even my money. That's a joke. Get it? I'm afraid your dad was a little rough on you. If he'd tried to get at the reasons behind the lies. . . . But people don't. I think I ought to go around lecturing at PTAs."

"I guess I feel better," Robby said.

"Remember what I said about being your ace in the hole?" Ivan asked. "I meant it. When I think the time is right, I *will* step in. Old Ivan's still got a few tricks in his bag."

"You mean you can do magic?" Robby asked.

"We'll see," Ivan said.

Just then Robby's mother called him to the telephone. It was Fatso Cotter.

"Listen, I heard you got in a fight," Fatso said. "I heard you even started it. And I wanted you to know I'm proud of you."

"How come you didn't invite me to your birthday party?" Robby asked.

"You didn't invite me to yours."

"But I didn't have a party," Robby said. "Just my folks and my sister and a cake."

"How was I supposed to know that?" Fatso asked. "I thought you had a party. Listen, did you get hurt much?"

"Naw," Robby said. "Well—some."

"Gee," Fatso said. "Listen, I'm sorry. And I'm sorry I didn't ask you to my party. I will next year, honest."

"You better," Robby said, "or you'll never get the present I bought you."

"THAT
MAKES SENSE!"

One afternoon Robby was doing his homework when Mrs. Glidden, who lived next door, dropped in and asked his mother if she would like to join a neighborhood bridge club.

"Oh, how sweet of you to ask me," Robby heard his mother say, "but unfortunately I don't play bridge."

Robby looked up from his history book. When Susan Jane and he had had the measles the year before, their parents had taught them how to play bridge, so of course his mother knew how to play bridge.

"My mother told a whopper," he said to Ivan when Mrs. Glidden had left and his mother was in the kitchen making dinner.

"Yes and no," Ivan said. "That's what you call a polite lie, like telling someone you just love her new dress when you really think it looks terrible. Your mother doesn't like Mrs. Glidden, so she doesn't want to be in a club with her. But she couldn't come right out and say, 'I don't like you,' could she?"

"Why not?"

"It would hurt Mrs. Glidden's feelings."

Robby nodded. "Just the same, I'm going to ask her about it. I'm going to ask her why it's all right for her to lie and not me."

"I wouldn't. You'd leave her without an answer, and a parent without an answer is on the spot. Does that make sense?"

"No."

"Let me put it this way," Ivan said. "A person without an answer will give you the world's longest answer. Figure *that* out. I'm so wise I ought to write

a book. Can you take dictation?"

"Do you mean my mom lied so Mrs. Glidden wouldn't cry?" Robby asked.

"Something like that."

"Then a lie not to hurt somebody's feelings isn't a bad lie."

"Not bad at all. Hardly even counts as a lie."

Robby thought. "Well, then, all I did was tell a polite lie about the fight. I didn't tell Mom and Dad I was in the fight because I didn't want to hurt their feelings."

And then, for the very first time, Ivan said, *"I don't believe you."*

"What did you say?" Robby cried.

"You heard me," Ivan said. He looked as if *he* might be going to cry. "You didn't tell them about the fight because you didn't want to get spanked. That's what you told me. It wouldn't have hurt their feelings; it would have hurt your seat, and you know it. So just now you told your first *real* lie. You lied to yourself."

"Ivan, you can't not believe me," Robby said. "You're the only person left that trusts me."

"Trust*ed*," Ivan said glumly. "When a person

starts lying to himself, they're done; it's downhill all the way. Not very grammatical, but true. And you know what comes next?"

"No," Robby said in a scared voice.

"The person can't tell the difference between truth and lying," Ivan said even more glumly. "What a future!"

"Ivan, I'll never do it again," Robby promised. "Cross my heart and hope to die. On my honor. On my *father's* honor."

"Don't do it for me," Ivan said. "Do it for yourself. You're the one that has to live with yourself. What a thought! I got that from Plato. I'm very well read. Now—if Australia were to come to the door right this minute and tell your mother her name was Australia, that would prove you hadn't lied. Right? Would it make you feel better if your mother knew you hadn't lied? Or is it enough that *you* know it? Don't answer till you've given it a lot of thought because this is where we separate the men from the boys."

Robby gave it a lot of thought.

"I guess you mean it ought to be enough that I know I'm not a liar," he said finally. "Like you said,

I know there's an Australia even if nobody in the whole world believes me. *Is* that what you mean, Ivan?"

"Exactly," Ivan said. "I'm proud of you. Mind like a steel trap."

"So I don't care if Australia comes to the door or not. Which she never will."

"Ha," Ivan said. "Don't bet on that. I told you old Ivan had a few tricks up his sleeve."

"You're a good friend, Ivan."

"Shucks," the parrot said modestly. "At least I have more to offer than 'Boy, have I got a hangover.' Seriously, I hope you'll run for President when you get old enough. We need honest men. I'd run myself, but they'd never elect a Russian."

"I better get through school first," Robby said.

At that moment the front doorbell rang, and Robby's mother answered it. Robby heard a familiar voice say, "You got any more brownies?"

"Brownies? What brownies? And who might you be?"

"Marvella Matilda Monica Follansbugle," the voice said. "But I'd rather be called Australia. I got it from a geography book."

"Oh, my goodness," Robby's mother said. "You're *real*."

"Huh?"

"Nothing," Robby's mother said. "I was just admiring your pearl earrings."

"Geez," Ivan said. "With a name like that, who could blame her? I wouldn't care if she called herself New Zealand."

"*That* makes sense," Robby laughed.

"I could have sworn I heard that bird say something," Robby's mother muttered.

About the Author

Isabel Langis Cusack was born in Berlin, New Hampshire, and ended up in Lantana, Florida, with many stops in between. She is a shell collector and a widely published short-story writer. *Ivan the Great* is her first book.